AMERICAN INSURRECTION

Written by Larry Corkins

DEDICATION

I dedicate this book to people everywhere who believe in equality for all, and in patriotism that includes all the people of the land. People who believe in the rights of all the citizens of their country and not a select few. Also, the integrity and justice for the people who defend the country they live in and not for the ones who attempt to overthrow their country so that they can repress certain colors and genders, because they don't like them. AKA January 6, 2021.

ACKNOWLEDGMENT

I want to acknowledge the Father, Son and Holy Spirit for giving me the wisdom and ability to write what some people cannot, but really want to say. And my Wife and children for heir undying support. Also, people everywhere who have been and continue to be kept down, repressed and even murdered just because they are not White and/or racist, or do not fit in the mold that hateful people want them to. Remember, even though this deals with very real historical events in America, it is still a work of fiction. Anything that resembles real life people is purely coincidental.

Prelude

On January 6, 2021, the sitting President who had only days until he was to be removed from office, insighted a riot against the Capitol of the United States of America in an attempt to stay in office. He kept lying to the American public about the idea in his head that he had actually won the Presidential race that he had in fact lost. On that day, the sitting Vice President was in the Capitol Building counting the Electoral College votes as ordered by the Constitution of the United States. The President made it clear to the racist people who came from all over America to be at the so-called rally (riot to overthrow the Government), that the Vice President, who had kept lying for the President for four years, was a traitor to him. He should be dealt with, which those ignorant racist people knew meant that he had to die. They even took a hangman's noose to kill him with, as they proceeded to attack the Capitol Building. All the while, the President who had just told them to go there and he would be there with them, went back to the White

House. It seems that those followers, aka mob, were very stupid, because the President who had told them minutes earlier that he was going with them actually lied to them, just as he had been doing for over five years. One year before being elected and the four years in the office. This story is about a group of racists who believed all of the President's lie and went to the Capitol to overthrow the Government of the United States, which is treason. Five people died that day, because of the President, but no one has ever held that President to account for their lives. He should be in prison for treason, but the justice system is broken and convicting racist White people is very hard to do in this country. All White people are not racist and the ones who are make it look bad for the ones who are not, but not as much as it makes it bad for Black people who get profiled, stopped and even killed by racist police, just for being Black. Who knows if there will ever be real justice for people of color, but we can keep praying and make changes in our own lives to stop doing those things that separate us all. Black Lives do matter, and no Black Lives Matter is not a racist or terrorist group as the then President kept telling his followers. He sounded like a modern-day Hitler, and still does.

Chapter 1

"Hey John, did you hear what the President said last night?" asked Tom, as he was walking into the racist Whites only bar that would frown on anyone who was not White coming in there. John turned to see who it was.

"Oh, hey Tom. No, I missed it. I was at the Klan rally last night. Why didn't you come?"

"I had something I had to do. I bet it was a good time though."

"Yeah, we hung that Black bitch Marris in effigy. Then we set her on fire."

"That's what I'm talking about. Fuck them Black mother fuckers."

"What did the President say?"

"Oh, he called Marris an ugly Black bitch in the last debate before the election."

"He said that on live tv?"

"He sure did."

"She deserved that. How dare she say that the entire country should be kind to each other. Fuck that. I ain't never being kind to any Black mother fucker."

"Me either. Fuck them."

"What else did he say?"

"He said his great-grandfather owned her great-grandmother and used to rape her ass every day."

"He got away with saying that truth?"

“Yep. Man, the media don’t give a fuck what he says on tv anymore. They like the ratings too much.”

“And he gets high ratings, because all the good people believe in him. Exclude all people who are not White. That’s his slogan and it works.”

“Yeah, it works because good ole boys and girls think the same way he does. Get the fuck out of our country if you ain’t White and on our side.”

“That’s right. Are you ready to vote him back in tomorrow?”

“Hell yeah. He ain’t going to get beat by that bitch. Like he said before, there are only good people on this side, the White side.”

"That's right. But make sure you vote, because I heard that everyone who hates Hisler is going to come out to vote Marris in."

"Those people got me fucked up. Hisler is the best President we ever had in this country. All the other Presidents tried to make Black people and Mexicans equal to us. Fuck that. Those people ain't shit. They can't even lick my boots."

"They can suck my dick though."

"Remember, Hisler said that all Mexicans are rapists and murderers and need to be deported to Mexico. And this time he is going to build ships to send all Black people back to Africa."

"But Black people are Americans now, not African. That is what they keep saying but fuck that. Send them anyway."

Just then, another White guy came into the bar. He was not known by anyone in the bar. He just stopped at the bar to get a drink. The other two men kept talking, and the new man could hear everything they were saying. He kept thinking to himself, “What the hell is wrong with these guys?” He finished his drink and started to leave, not wanting to hear anymore shit coming out of their mouths.

Tom noticed a look he gave over their way as he was leaving. “You got a problem?” he asked.

The man did not respond. John could hear the silence of his non-response, so he got up and stepped in front of the man. “Are you deaf, man?” he asked.

The man just looked at John in his face and said, “Excuse me.”, as he pushed John out of his way. John took offence right away and swung on the man. The man ducked but swung back knocking out two of John’s teeth. Tom jumped in and the man got beat up pretty badly. After they beat him up, they drug him outside and left him on the curb.

Tom and John went back into the bar. A little while later, two police officers came into the bar with the man who got beat up and arrested Tom and John for battery. They both posted bail the next day and had court dates set. When they went to court, they both got fined and had to do community service. The judge did not impose any jail time, which did not seem right to the man who had been beat p by the two.

Nothing he could do.

Chapter 2

Election day: Record numbers of people were coming out to vote. In the early returns, it was favoring the President Ron Hisler, but there were a lot of votes still to be counted, including the mail-in ballots. It was going to be a while before there would be a winner.

Racist White people, and stupid people of other colors who bought into lies from the President that their own race wasn't shit were voting in record numbers. Former Vice President Kamilla Marris was also expecting a record number of people to vote for her. It was really coming down to racist White people and stupid people vs. everyone else. It seemed that the President underestimated White people who were not racist and all people of every other color turning out to vote for Marris. By the end of the night, Marris had won the election by a lot, even though they both had record numbers of voters for them. Marris not only won the electoral college votes by a landslide, but she had also won the popular vote by a lot.

As for following protocol and excepting your defeat, Hisler would not concede, but instead claimed that he had won. He accused everyone of rigging the election and said there was widespread voter fraud. All lies and everyone knew it, but the racist people in Congress went along with it anyway.

Chapter 3

Kamilla Marris won the election and was about to be the first woman President in the history of the United States. President Hisler went on every tv show and news channel to keep claiming that he won the election and that it was stolen from him. His followers believed him, just like cult followers do.

Even earlier in the year when COVID hit the United States, President Hisler told people that they just needed to drink bleach and put lights inside their bodies, sounding like a complete and total moron. Some dumbass people actually did it too. Of course, they ended up in the hospital or dead, but Hisler did not care. See, one thing his dumb followers never realized is that he never gave a fuck about them. He was just using stupid people to further his own agenda. When other people would tell those stupid people that Hisler was nuts and just using them, they would defend him like dumbass people do.

The Vice President knew that they had lost, but when he told the President that he needed to stop lying about the outcome of the election, the President yelled at him and accused him of helping them cheat him out of his victory. Tom believed that Hisler was really honest and did not believe that Marris won the election. He started posting lies on Facebook about how Black people and their lovers stole the election from the greatest President ever.

John did the same, as if they were sharing the same mind. There was even a group of racist White people who called themselves the Loud Boys. They were a racist group like the Ku Klux Klan. They had people go to non-violent rallies for the Black Lives Matter movement and start trouble with the police and act like it was the Black Lives Matter members who started it. President Hisler was behind that too, by saying on tv that Black Lives Matter was a hate group and terrorists, which could not be further from the truth.

Unnoticed by just about everyone, President Hisler took some of the defense spending money and gave it to a company to make huge ships, so that when he got back in office, he could declare martial law and have everyone who was black round up and placed on those ships, while being bound by chains like slavery days. His plan was then to send all those people to Africa, but not really. If he took the Black people to Africa, they would just come back fighting, so instead, his real plan was to put them on the ships, take them out to the middle of the ocean and throw all of them overboard to drown or be eaten by sharks. The ships would then come back and get more Black people, until all the black people were gone from this country. His plan for Mexican Americans was to just take them to the boarder and shoot all of them, claiming they were trying to enter the United States illegally, even though most of them always lived here. All of his plans would not come to fruition if he could not be President anymore, so he kept lying about losing.

Chapter 4

Christmas came and went and so did New Year's Day. It was now January 2, 2021. President Hisler was determined that he would stay in power. He badgered the Vice President to do the right thing, according to him, and change the electoral votes on January 6, when he counts them in Congress. The Vice President would not do that, because he knew Hisler was lying and he was very faithful to the Constitution of the United States.

President Hisler was on the phone all day on the 2nd of January, trying anything he could to get someone to help him with his lies. The Racist Party in Congress was still lying for him, but the other Party was not going to let those lies change things. Hisler called his staff into the Oval Office on the 3rd day of January and told them they had to help him come up with an idea to stay in power, but no one could do that, plus they all knew that he had really lost the election.

As the meeting ended in a heated debate between the President and the Vice President, the staff walked out of the Oval Office talking to each other about how crazy the President was and saying they could not wait until his tenure was over in a couple of weeks so that they could get away from him.

Meanwhile Tom and John, staunch followers of the President were trying to figure a way to help the President keep his job. As they were doing this, they saw online that the President was telling his followers to come to the Capitol on January 6th for a rally, to support him staying in office. Everyone of his followers knew that meant they were about to overthrow the Government of the Untied States. Tom and John were ready to go, so they planned out their trip and encouraged other racist idiots to go too.

Chapter 5

January 4th had come, and President Hisler was getting mad more and more by the moment. Not just mad, angry, but mad as in crazy. He was losing it, because he had promised White people who supported him that he would get rid of Black people and Hispanics, so that they could live without having to worry about crime, like White people don't commit crimes every day.

"What are you going to do when the shit hits the fan on the sixth?" asked Hisler's Chief of Staff.

"I'm going to watch my people take our country back, like in the days of slavery," Hisler exclaimed.

“Do you really think that you are going to get away with that?”

“Fuck yeah. People are stupid and they’ll do anything I want them to do. Why do you think no one has succeeded in stopping me?”

“I really don’t know.”

“I can sell horse shit to a chef, like it’s a delicacy.’

“Those people believe in you, but you are throwing them to the wolves, sir.”

“I don’t give a fuck about them. They believe that I do and that is going to keep working as long as I say what they want to hear. You see how I told people to drink bleach and those dumb mother fuckers did it,” laughed Hisler.

“I thought you believed that”

“Fuck no. You think I’m really that stupid? But they are.”

“So, you’re going to trick and lie to your followers to get them to overthrow the government for you, so you can stay in office?”

“Hell yeah!”

“That’s treason, sir,” explained the Chief of Staff.

“Who gives a fuck! They ain’t going to do shit to me, because I have the Republicans on my side, and they are all stupid as fuck!”

“Why do you say that?”

“I hate people who are not like me, but so do they. That’s how I became President in the first place. They all want Black people and Mexicans to go move somewhere else. When I take back the Presidency, I am going to declare martial law and impose a new agenda, where I will be King, and I will rule until I die. Congress will be dissolved and only I will say what is what," explained Hisler.

"You're crazy as hell!"

"No, I'm running this bitch and when I am in charge, I'm giving this country to Russia and my friend Putin, and he is going to let me stay on as King of America."

"What the fuck?"

Hisler pushed a button on his desk and told his secretary to have Secret Service come into the Oval Office.

They came in and Hisler said, “Take this fool and put him somewhere where no one can find him.”

They took the Chief of Staff away, kicking and screaming.

“You’ll never get away with this!” the Chief of Staff yelled, as they forced him to go with them.

Chapter 6

January 5th, 2021. President Hisler made the final arrangements to have a mob, or rally at the Capitol. After that, he had lunch with his wife, who hates him.

"How are you going to overthrow the government?" asked Mrs. Hisler, "You can't do that. They're not going to let you do that."
"Who's not going to let me do that? I will do what the fuck I want, bitch. Don't forget that I can just send your ass back to Russia or the middle of the ocean, if I want. You do what the fuck I say or else," Hisler exclaimed.

Mrs. Hisler was very upset, but she knew better than to say anything else. She didn't say another word while finishing her lunch.

After lunch, President Hisler made some phone calls to fans of his. His followers were not just followers of his who loved him on a reality show that he used to be on before he ran for President. They were fans. They were all racist or just plain stupid, because if they were not White, then he did not like them at all. His goal was to get into office for a second term to finish what he started as far as take out all the Black and Hispanic people or just simply send them elsewhere.

Hisler called in the Vice President, to tell him that he had to throw out the electoral votes and change them to votes for him. Once again, the Vice President said that he would never do that. President Hisler was boiling mad, but the Vice President did not care. He was going to abide by the Constitution, not a nutcase who was hungry for more power.

Chapter7

January 6, 2021. This was the day of the insurrection of the Capitol Building of the United States of America. President Hisler was all set to take his rightful place as King Dictator of the United States of America. Of course, that was all in his mind, but he was about to try and make it happen for real, even though it was crazy as hell, just like him.

Racist people were everywhere. They were getting off of buses, pulling up in cars, trucks, etc. and even walking to the place where President Hisler had designated for them to be. The mob was in full affect to try and overthrow the Government of the United States. They were homegrown terrorists, about to commit treason.

Several Racist people spoke at the so-called rally. It was really an insurrection. President Hisler was the last speaker. He told his usual lies about how he won the election, and his opponent was falsely given the victory. His racist followers did not care about the truth, they just wanted Hisler to stay in power so that he would get rid of all the people who were different than them. It begged the question, "How could this happen in America?" The answer was it was happening.

"At the Capitol Building, the Vice President has turned against us and needs to be dealt with! He is a traitor to good patriotic Americans like you! In the past traitors were hung until dead! I need you to go to the Capitol Building and fight like hell until I am King of this bitch! Go now, I will go there with you!" Hisler lied to everyone there.

The mob of racist unpatriotic Americans rushed, ran down to the Capitol Building because their racist treasonous leader said to. After all, he said he would meet them there. He lied! He went back to the White House and acted like nothing was happening.

The mob of racist people stormed the Capitol Building, waving American flags, shouting things like "Hang the Vice President!"

It was a horrible scene. The Vice President had to be hidden from the mob that wanted him to die. Senators and Representatives of every state had to hide for the safety of their own lives. Police were hurt, because they could not stop the mob. The Vice President called in the National Guard, which is not even his job to do.

The mob rushed into offices and even the Chambers of Congress. They broke windows and stole things. They hurt many people. They did not care as long as in their minds they were right. The President was on their side and that was all that mattered.

Chapter 8

When the smoke had cleared, the mob was dispersed and the Capitol Building was finally secured, the entire world was in shock by what had happened that day. The President of the

United States of America had waged a war against his own government and acted like he had nothing to do with it.

Five people died that day, but instead of charging the President who had total blame for causing the deaths of those people, the Justice Department did nothing to him. He was guilty of treason, but no one seemed to care. He lost the election and had to get out of office, but to this day he is still not held accountable for his actions and causing the deaths of those five people. He was seemingly untouchable and racism in America was given a pass by the Government who is supposed to protect everyone, no matter what color or creed or race you are. Apparently, the White men and women in Congress were okay with people dying for the great cause of lies and racism of one man.

"Ring! Ring! Ring!" an alarm went off and a man woke up thinking, "Wow, I just had the most unbelievable nightmare!" That couldn't have really happened. A President who swore to uphold the Constitution of the United States threw a pitty-party for himself that resulted in full, fledged treason against the very Country he swore to protect? And got away with it? It is a good thing that it did not really happen, as the new Adolf Hitler described those terrorists who formed that mob, as good patriots!

After all, there is nothing more patriotic than destroying your own Government and killing innocent people, just so one man can use your dumbass to help himself become a dictator!

Prologue

This is a work of fiction, just like some people's lies are. If something like this ever happened, then all I can say id, "God, help us all!"

www.ingramcontent.com/pod-product-compliance
Ingram Content Group UK Ltd.
Pitfield, Milton Keynes, MK11 3LW, UK
UKHW040014200726
13854UKWH00001B/191

9 798439 882434